ALWAYS *with* YOU

Part One

by

M. LEIGHTON

Cash will forever be in my heart. He is, after all, just like my husband in all the ways that matter. Thank God for men like him!

ONE

Olivia

I CURL my fingers into the neck of my shirt as I slide down the back of the closed bathroom door. My brain is running in circles trying to make sense of what just happened, but it seems to be the slowest of my organs. My heart is pounding, my lungs are heaving and every muscle and nerve in my entire body is trembling, I think.

I close my eyes and fight back tears. When a soft knock thuds on the door behind me, I don't even move. It's all I can do to get my voice back online.

"Just a minute," I say in as normal a tone as I can muster.

"It's me, babe. Can I come in?"

My chest squeezes painfully, protectively around my aching heart. "C-can you give me just a minute?"

"Yes, I'll give you a minute. I'd give you the world if you asked me for it. You know that, right?"

My eyes burn like fire. "Yes, I know that," I force out, even though I feel doubtful and betrayed at the moment.

There's a pause, during which I hear nothing on the other side of the door. I know Cash is still there. Not only have I not heard him walk off, but I can *feel* him through the wooden barrier, like heat beckoning my cold soul toward it.

And then I hear his quiet words. "I love you, Olivia Davenport. You're the most important person in my life. Now. Always."

Tears spill from between my tightly-closed lids. "I-I love you, too."

"Please let me in. I want to hold you. I *need* to hold you."

I'm just starting to push to my feet when I hear another familiar voice. I smile through my tears.

"Move it, sweetie. This is best friend territory. I'll come get you when it's all clear." Cash makes no response, but I can imagine him glaring at Ginger. I hear a soft rustling sound followed by Ginger's hushed, "God, what are you made of? Lead?"

She's probably trying to push him out of her way, which wouldn't be easy. Not even for a large man would that be an easy task. Cash is still a six foot-five inch wall of broad chest, thick arms, strong legs and lean muscle.

"I'm not leaving until she lets me in," Cash says, determination hardening his voice.

"Just let me talk to her first. Trust me. It's better this way. Now out of my way, Thor."

I hear a grunt and then the doorknob rattles. "Liv, let me in. I've got something very important to tell you," Ginger says. I know it's a ruse, but honestly, I'd rather talk to her for a minute before I see Cash anyway. Somebody needs to talk me down off this ledge of insecurity.

I reach up and twist the lock, leaning away from the door just enough that Ginger can open it a crack and squeeze through. She immediately closes and locks it, then slides down to sit on the floor beside me.

"Phew! Got my workout trying to move the barbarian out of the way. He was *not* to keen on letting me in here first."

"Yeah, I heard."

She turns to look at me. "He's over the moon for you, you realize that, right?"

I nod hesitantly.

"I mean, the guy doesn't even look at my ass when I walk by. He's definitely off the market."

I smile a little. "Is that the true test of a man's level of taken-ness?"

She frowns as though my question is absurd. "Of course. What hot-blooded man wouldn't at least take a peek at a world class ass as it goes by?"

"Blind ones?"

"Exactly!" she replies emphatically. "Blind ones or extremely taken ones. Hell, even gay men look at my ass. I mean, have you *seen* my ass?"

"As a matter of fact I have. It's quite dazzling."

"See? And you're a straight, *taken* woman. It's irresistible." She shrugs. "Just the way it is."

"Is that what you had to tell me that's so important?"

"No, I was pretty sure you already knew that."

I nod. When she doesn't continue, I prompt. "Well?"

"Oh, I just wanted to tell you that Sophie is a conniving whore and we can't trust her."

Although I *love* Ginger's assessment of her, I wonder what makes her feel that way, other than womanly solidarity.

"What makes you say that?"

She shrugs again. "Intuition I suppose. Something about her…those eyes maybe. I can tell she's up to something. Something *not good.*"

"But what?"

"I can't be sure yet, but the most obvious thing would be that she wants your man."

My heart stutters in my chest. "And do you think that's possible?"

Please say no! Please say no!

My gut tells me that Cash is mine—heart and soul, always and forever. Like I am his. But this whole thing with being unable to get pregnant has my emotions in such turmoil, my heart isn't as certain as it once was. I feel so insecure. So inadequate. Like I've disappointed him, even though he's told me a thousand and one times that his life will be perfect, with or without a baby.

But thinking about the look on his face when he saw Sophie…when he saw the little girl, Isabella…

My stomach rolls over in a bout of nausea.

Ginger sits up and grabs my arm. "Hell. No. That boy is so in love with you, I'm envious. Me! The girl of no-strings-attached, hot sex. What you two have makes *me* want it, too. And I wouldn't want it if it wasn't extraordinary." She settles back against the door before she continues. "I mean, do you think I'd take *this* off the market for anything less than the true, deep, everlasting kind of love? I couldn't do that to humanity and feel good about it."

She says this with a straight face. Totally Ginger. I have to laugh, even though my heart doesn't feel better yet.

"I realize that's a big deal and I really hope you can find it one day. It's only fair that *you* feel this kind of misery as well."

Ginger sighs. "I don't know if I'll ever find what you have."

"Why don't you just ask him out for God's sake?"

"Who?"

I give her a withering look. "Don't even pretend that we're not *both* talking about Gavin."

"He's not interested, Liv, I'm telling ya." My best friend has tried to blow off her interest in Gavin, but I can tell by her expression that it hurts her. I've thought all along that she really likes Gavin. Like, more than just a fling. Nothing has ever happened, though.

"I think you're wrong. That pat on the ass he gave you earlier was anything but disinterested. What does he have to do, take you into a dark corner and rip your clothes off?"

"Preferably."

"I think you should go for it. What do you have to lose?"

Ginger closes her eyes and leans her head back against the thick wood of the door. "My heart. I...I don't think I want just a fling with him."

This admission is hard for my friend, which is why she isn't looking at me. She's unaccustomed to tenderness or unexpected weakness. She's always been in charge, in complete control, and I'm sure this is a foreign feeling for her.

"Maybe he doesn't either, but there's only one way to find out."

"And if it's a bust?" she asks, her voice low and somber.

"I've survived broken hearts. You will, too. They're all worth it when you find the real thing. The right one."

She opens her eyes and pins me with her stare. "Like what you have with Cash?"

My stomach flips over. "Yes, like what I have with Cash."

"You realize that nothing will ever come between you two unless you let it, right?"

I look into my friend's wise blue eyes. "So don't let it, is that what you're saying?"

"That's exactly what I'm saying. He loves you, Liv. And you love him. This is just a bump in the road. Don't make it into something it's not. He didn't marry her. He married *you*."

"But they have a child together," I remind her, my throat closing over the words even as I utter them.

"They *might* have a child together. I still don't believe it," she says stubbornly.

8

"Did you see her eyes? Those are Davenport eyes."

"I hate to be the one to tell you, Liv, but there are other men in the world with dark brown eyes."

"But they're almost black. Just like Cash's."

"And there are other almost-black eyes in the world, too. Don't jump to conclusions. And even if it is, so what? So he has a kid with someone else. That changes nothing unless you let it. You can still have babies with him. Little black-eyed babies that he'll get to hold when they're born and watch grow up. This woman has nothing on you, Liv. Not one damn thing."

"If you could just convince my heart of that."

"That's not my job. That's your husband's. And he's already trying to do that. You just have to let him."

"What do you mean?"

"He made her leave right after you excused yourself."

"He did?"

"He did. Said he'd talk to her later, that he needed to check on you."

Even though it's rude and inconsiderate to ask her to leave when she's really done nothing wrong (not technically), it makes me feel good that Cash did that for me.

"And don't you dare say that was rude of him, Miss Southern Hospitality."

My mouth drops open. "I wasn't... I didn't..." She knows me far too well.

"You were gonna. But it *wasn't* rude. She interrupted. Dropped by unannounced. To drop the mother of all bombs. At Christmas, no less. Sweet baby Jesus, who does that?" When I don't answer, Ginger shakes her head. "No decent person. Which means she's obviously dumb as a box of hair. Makes me wonder if the little girl is that stupid. If she is, I feel even sorrier for Cash. I mean, who wants an idiot for a daughter?"

I smile again. Ginger is good for me.

I throw in with her. Not because it's right, but because it just makes me feel better.

"Right? And what if she won't work when she grows up? What if she's really lazy and she just wants to live in the basement of the new house until she's fifty?"

"A basement-dwelling fifty year old— every father's dream. Hell, she might even be toothless by that point. They look like two women who are prone to dental hygiene problems, don't you think?"

At this, I laugh outright. Both Sophie and Isabella look clean and neat and nowhere near the vicinity of having bad dental hygiene, but I love the picture Ginger paints. Although completely unrealistic, it somehow soothes me to think of them this way. At least for a few minutes. Until my poor heart can recover from being devastated by the two beautiful interlopers.

"I love you, Ginger," I tell my friend.

"I love you, too, Livie. And if you want to become lesbians and run away from this mess, I'll consider it, but only after I've had a run at Gavin. Deal?"

"Deal."

She leans over to kiss my cheek before she stands and practically pushes me across the floor when she opens the door.

"Your turn, Thor!" she calls out. She glances back at me long enough to wink before she disappears and the door closes again.

I'm ready for Cash to come to me now. I'm ready to feel his arms around me. I'm ready to feel his lips brush my temple. I'm ready to hear him tell me he loves me and that I'm the only one. I'm ready to hear that more than anything.

TWO

Cash

GINGER GIVES me a thumb's up when I pass her on the way to Olivia. When I reach the bathroom door, I twist the knob and push. I feel resistance against it, so I push, slow and hard, until I can get it open enough to make it through. I'm a big guy. I can't squeeze through a damn crack like Ginger.

Once inside, I look down into my wife's pale face and my anger returns. Damn Sophie and her unexpected appearance!

Without a word, I bend, scooping Olivia into my arms and then turning to sit against the door like she was, cradling her against my chest. I brush my lips over her forehead.

I think of the best way forward, taking into consideration the way Olivia's mind works and what she needs most from me. My guess is reassurance. I know this was a blow to her. Probably not Sophie as much as the little girl. But I want her to know where I stand with both of them. If not for *her* peace of mind, then for *mine.* This woman is more important to me than anything. When she hurts, I hurt.

"When I was in junior high, Dad got us a dog. We'd wanted one for a while. I guess he got tired of us asking him about it, so he broke over and got a hound dog. Named him Stanley. Nash and I were both into comics at the time. We figured it was better to combine Stan and Lee rather than giving our dog two names, so we agreed on Stanley. Stanley was a great dog. Smart, fast. Drooled all over the place, but the only one who cared about that was Mom. It didn't take long for him to become a member of the family. Stanley Davenport.

"About three years later, Stanley got the neighbor's new dog pregnant. She had pups and we got the pick of the litter since Stanley was the father. We were into sports by then, so we named that dog Heisman. He was cute as hell at eight weeks when we got him. I loved him immediately. Something about seeing him when he was born, about knowing that he was part Stanley's, it's like he was family from the first breath he took. Seeing him grow up from just a pup, watching him through those gawky, all-legs months...he was almost human. Or at least it felt like it. I got so attached to him, he even slept on the end of my bed most nights. I loved Stanley. He was still a member of the family, but Heisman was *mine*. He felt like mine more than Stanley did. I watched him grow up. I taught him tricks and held him on the way to the vet for his shots. We were part of each other's life in a different way than Stanley. We were all family, of course, but there was just something special about Heisman."

I glance down at Olivia. She's staring up at me, her bright green eyes shining. If I'd given it more thought, I might not have used a couple of dogs as analogies for real children. I guess I just want to make her feel better so much that I'd say just about anything. Including telling her some boring story about my childhood animals.

"I'd be able to love any kid of mine, but I won't lie and say that a child *with you* wouldn't be different. Because it would. The love I have for you...watching *our baby* grow in your belly...seeing it come into the world...hearing it say 'Daddy' for the first time...there are few things in life I could love more than that. But you're one of them. If we are blessed with a baby, I'll love it like my own flesh. If we're not, it won't make me love you any less. Or love another child any more. There's a place in me...way down here," I tell her, thumping the center of my chest with my fist, "that's reserved for you and our baby. Nothing else can ever live there. Just you. And our child. If we don't have a baby of our own, all of this will just be yours because you are my whole world. Nothing and *no one* will ever change that. Do you hear me, Olivia Davenport? Nothing. And no one. Ever."

She nods, her big, glassy eyes filling with tears. "I needed this. I needed *you.*"

"I know. That's why I made her leave and came back here. I could feel your heart breaking like an earthquake. Once the shock wore off, I just wanted her out of here so I could get to you. You'll always be the most important person in any room."

"I have to be adult about this, though. I have to come to terms with the possibility that we might not be able to have children of our own. But that doesn't mean you can't enjoy an unexpected child."

"*If* she's mine."

"*If* she's yours," she agrees.

"You know I'll do whatever you want, right?"

"I know. And I know that *you know* that I could never, *would never* ask you not to participate in your child's life, no matter who the mother is."

As much as I hate how hurtful this is for her, and how hard it will be for her, I never doubted that Olivia would do the right thing. Not once.

"I *do* know that. Your compassion is one of the things I love most about you. I know you would never hold a child's birth circumstance against it."

"No, I couldn't do that. No matter how much I'd like to."

"*Wanting to* makes you human. *Refusing to* makes you Olivia."

"Cash, please be patient with me. Knowing the right thing and doing the right thing still doesn't make it easy to do the right thing. And lately, I've been so...so..."

I can see by the line between her eyebrows that distress is setting back in. "I know, baby. I know. I wish I could take it away. All of it. All of the stress and the disappointment and the doubt. And I'm doing everything I can to make you feel loved, no matter what happens."

"I know you are. It's just...it's just hard."

"That doesn't mean we'll stop trying, though. None of this changes anything. Not really."

"I hope not. I really, really hope not."

The dejected note in her voice reminds me that no matter how brave and resolute her words, there is still a rough road ahead for my wife. And there's little I can do to change it.

THREE

Olivia

I FEEL somewhat better when I wake. Cash is still asleep next to me and his body heat radiates toward me much like his love does, which has been hitting me full force since the moment he stepped into the bathroom last night.

We eventually made our way back to the Christmas celebration. Sophie and her surprise visit never made it back into the conversation, for which I was very thankful, but I could tell by the sympathetic looks and all the spontaneous hugs I got that everyone was feeling sorry for the fragile Olivia. I guess it's no secret to anyone now that I'm having difficulty conceiving. At least everyone, including my mean and outspoken mother, had the good grace and common courtesy not to mention it.

I found a nice respite for my worries in watching Ginger. I've never seen her engage in casual, cautious flirtation before. It was quite interesting. It was equally interesting to see Gavin turn on his full charm. Maybe he'd thought she wasn't interested in him. Or maybe he was keeping a distance out of respect for Cash and me. I don't know, but whatever his reasons for keeping that distance, they evaporated last night. I make a mental note to call Ginger later and see if she slept alone last night. She and Gavin were the last to leave and they walked out together, so it's hard to tell.

Once we got back to the apartment that we're still staying in behind the office, Cash undressed me sweetly, carried me to bed and spooned me until I was fast asleep. I thought at first that we might make love, but another failed attempt to create a child wouldn't have been a good fit for me today, so I have to give props to my intuitive husband for not pressing the matter.

The phone rings, shattering the early morning quiet. Cash groggily reaches for his phone, his voice muffled by the pillow as he speaks into it.

"What?"

I listen to Cash's end of the conversation, my curiosity rising with each word.

"She what?"

"In *this* parking lot?"

"Why the hell didn't she tell me she had no money and nowhere to go?"

My heart sinks. I don't have to hear both voices to know who's being discussed. And if this woman, who Cash obviously knew intimately some years ago, and her child, who she claims is Cash's, don't have a place to go, that can only mean that my life is about to get even harder. Even more complicated.

"Fine. I'll take care of it. Thanks for the head's up, man."

Cash tosses his phone back on the nightstand with a loud clatter and then rolls onto his back. He throws his arm over his eyes and I can see the muscle along his jawline twitching rhythmically. When Cash grits his teeth, his temper is stirring to life. And he's definitely gritting his teeth.

"That was Gavin," he says in a low growl. "Evidently Sophie has no money and nowhere to go, so she and the little girl slept in her car in the parking lot last night."

I say nothing. I don't know what *to* say.

"What the hell kind of mother makes her kid sleep in a car in the parking lot of a damn bar?"

I don't answer because he already knows the answer.

A crappy one.

Angrily, Cash whips back the covers and leaps from the bed to stalk to the bathroom. I lie quietly and patiently to await his return. It's only seconds later that the door reopens, though, and my husband walks back to the bed. He perches one hip on the side of the mattress and leans over me, brushing his lips back and forth across mine before trailing them to my ear.

"Good morning, my beautiful wife," he murmurs.

"Good morning, my handsome husband," I reply, winding my arms around his neck.

"Can't we just rewind to yesterday?"

"How I wish we could," I tell him candidly.

He leans up to look down into my face, his gorgeous black eyes glinting like onyx in the soft wedge of light pouring from the bathroom. "I wish I could skip every day that would hurt you. Make your life perfect. All the time."

"No one's life is perfect, but as long as I have you, it's as perfect as I need it to be."

"Well, you don't have to worry about that. You're never getting rid of me."

"That's the best news I've heard all day."

"It's only a little after seven."

"Then tell me again tonight. I'll say the same thing."

"Gladly," he says, giving me a hard peck before he moves away. "I'm going to splash some water on my face and then go out and see what's going on. Do you wanna come with me?"

"No, I think I'll stay here."

"I won't be long," he promises.

I try to give him a bright smile when he comes out of the bathroom, dressed in last night's clothes with his hair still sticking up at odd angles all over his head, but nothing in my heart feels bright. Something tells me that there's a sob story on its way. And that that sob story is going to turn my life upside down.

Again.

FOUR

Cash

SOPHIE IS watching me as I walk to the only car in the lot. It's a total piece of shit black hatchback that looks like it's being held together with duct tape. I don't see a license tag in the front and I can't help wondering if she drove that thing all the way down here from Canada.

Or if she's been living somewhere else all this time. Like in the states. Where she could reach me fairly easily. To let me know she's okay or, I don't know, to tell me I have a damn kid that I've missed for nine years. Just thinking about it puts fire in my blood.

I walk to the driver's side just as she's rolling down the window.

"What are you doing here, Sophie?" I ask, my tone admittedly clipped.

I feel like a shitheel when her eyes fill with tears. "I'm so sorry to be here, Cash. This way. After all this time. But...but I just have nowhere else to go and...and...I need help. *We* need help."

I glance in the back seat at the little girl curled up on her side, hands folded under one rosy cheek, a blanket pulled all the way up to her neck.

"Why the hell didn't you tell me that last night? Jesus Christ, Sophie! She'll catch her death sleeping in a car!"

I move to yank open the back door and gently extricate the sleeping Isabella. She curls toward me, snuggling against my chest. A pang of paternal protectiveness mixed with fury at Sophie burn in my gut.

I kick the door shut with my boot and speak to my ex as I pass. "Let's take this inside where it's warm." I don't wait to see if she follows me.

Within seconds, I hear the slam of another door and the scrambling of feet on gravel as Sophie rushes to catch up to my long, angry stride.

"You have every right to be upset with me, Cash, but at least let me explain."

"Explain," I reply, still walking.

"Wait," Sophie says, tugging on my arm. "Not in there."

I stop and turn to look at her. "Why not?"

Her blue eyes, eyes I used to think were quite beautiful, plead with mine. "Because I...I doubt you're alone."

I frown. "Of course I'm not alone. My wife is in there, but why does that matter?"

Sophie casts her eyes downward and then left to right before she hesitantly drags them back up to mine. "She...I...does she know about me? About us?"

"She does now."

"Does she know...*everything*?"

I let her squirm in the quiet, in the discomfort of my pointed stare for several long seconds before I answer. "No, but she will."

"Cash, please. Please don't tell her. Can't we just put all that behind us and find some way to move forward? To start over? Not for me, but for Isabella?"

I glance down at the bundle I'm carrying. What if this really *is* my child?

"Let's just take this one step at a time. Starting with going inside. Olivia is part of my present...*the biggest* part of my present, so she *will* be involved. Maybe we can let the past be the past, but if there's any kind of future for us, she'll be with me."

"I totally understand that," Sophie says, nodding vigorously. "And I'm happy for you,

Cash. Truly. I don't want to cause problems for you. For either of you."

"Good. Then don't."

"I won't, I won't. But...don't let her be mean to my little girl."

"Be mean to your little girl?" Fury sweeps through me. "Let me tell you something. Olivia is one of the kindest, most considerate people you could ever hope to meet. She would never, *ever* be mean to a kid, for God's sake. And I can tell you one thing for damn sure: If we had a daughter, she sure as shit wouldn't be found asleep in the backseat of car."

I stop myself before I get nasty. I need to at least keep *some amount* of peace, just in case this woman is the mother of my child.

Sophie has the good grace to blush and the good sense to keep her mouth shut. She nods once and releases my arm so that I can carry Isabella into the club where it's warm.

Looks like it's gonna be one helluva morning.

FIVE

Olivia

I HEAR Cash's low voice much sooner than I expected and my heart stutters. I raise my head from the pillow to hear him better. That's when I realize he's not speaking to me.

"Wait for us at the bar," he tells someone in a stilted tone. Likely Sophie, if I had to guess.

Wait for us.

Us.

That means she isn't gone. That means I won't be able to avoid this like I'd wanted to.

Some part of me, irrational though it is, was hoping that Cash would go outside, discover that this whole Isabella thing was a ruse, get angry and send them both packing. Minutes later, he'd come back to bed, to *me*, and we could resume the relatively drama-free life we've been enjoying and focus on trying to get me pregnant. That was the plan. And I liked that plan.

But that was wishful thinking on my part, no doubt.

Something tells me that Sophie won't be nearly that easy to get rid of. Not that I should want to, really. I mean, if she's the mother of Cash's child then I should get used to seeing her on occasion, right? I should want for them to get along for the sake of his daughter, right?

His daughter.

My heart breaks a little bit all over again. Some woman…some random woman from Cash's past, has waltzed right into our lives and given him the one thing that I can't. Without even trying. Just like that. So easy. Even if I am able to get pregnant eventually, this stranger will have stolen so much from us. She'll have given Cash so many firsts—his first child, his first daughter, the first person to call him "Daddy." Together, they'll share a year of firsts of all sorts—first New Year, first Easter, first Independence Day, first birthday, first Thanksgiving, first Christmas. Cash will be a father for the first time on all of those days. And the mother of his child won't be me. And the child won't be ours. I don't know how *not* to be devastated about that. It's the one thing that I wanted most to give him. To share with him. For us to do together. As husband and wife. Then as a mother and a father.

Nausea flourishes in my stomach like blooms of algae on a pond's surface. I feel sickly green from the inside out.

I'm lying on my side with my face turned into the pillow when I hear Cash quietly open the door and step inside. Instantly, I feel his presence surround me. It's like he changes the way the air moves, the way the sounds travel. My entire universe shifts on its axis when he's near. It tilts in his direction, like he's my sun. Because he is. My world revolves around him. And his used to revolve around me. But now there are other planets in the rotation. Foreign bodies in our solar system. It's not just Cash and me anymore. And if this little girl really is his, it will never be just Cash and me ever again. And that breaks my heart, too.

He sighs as he slides onto the mattress beside me, his hand finding its way to my hip as though it's meant to be there, as though when he's near, he has to be touching me. I know what that feels like because I feel the same way around him.

"Is everything okay?" I ask hesitantly.

He scrubs his other hand over his face. It's something he does when he's agitated. And I know he must be. All this has to be weighing on him.

"I don't know. I don't know what the hell to think. I only know that whatever this is, however this unfolds, I need you by my side. We're in this together. Right?"

The way he said it—*Right?*—brings my protective instincts roaring to the surface. Could it be that this big, strong, beautiful, capable man thinks that this could cause him to lose me?

The thought is ludicrous. But so, so sweet I could cry.

I roll up onto my knees and take Cash's face between my hands. "We are in *everything* together. As long as you want me around, I'm here. Right by your side. Got it?"

I hold his sparkling black eyes as they search mine. There's a sadness in them that mirrors what's in my heart. "This isn't the way it was supposed to happen," he says softly.

My throat squeezes and my eyes burn. "I know," I manage to eke out.

"I don't want you to think that because she's an old friend, that because she says this little girl is mine, that it changes anything between us."

"I won't," I assure him. But I know I'll have to remind myself of that fact a million times before this is over.

"Will you come out and talk to her with me? The little girl is still asleep. I put her on the couch in the office."

"Of course I will. Just let me clean up a bit."

I press my lips to his just before he pulls me into his arms for a bone-crushing hug. It's as though he wants to imprint his body, his love, his certainty onto my skin in a permanent way.

"Take your time. I'll wait," he says when he releases me. I get up and make my way slowly toward the bathroom. Cash holds onto my hand and then my fingers, right down to the very tips, until I take the step that separates us completely. The instant that small contact is broken, I feel bereft and oddly afraid, as though everything that was so solid two days ago is now as fragile as the most delicate of crystal.

I'm near tears again by the time I close the bathroom door. I go immediately to the sink to splash cold water on my face in hopes that *that woman* won't see that I'm upset. I can't show the slightest weakness. I get the feeling she'd exploit the hell out of it. I have no reason to think that, of course. Other than my strong and instant dislike of her. It's not worth risking, though, so I'll keep my strong face on, just in case.

When my hair is brushed, my teeth are brushed and I'm feeling a little less…off kilter, I rejoin my husband, who is pacing the room like a caged lion when I open the door.

I walk right over to him, lace my fingers through his and smile my biggest smile.

"Ready?"

He stares at me for a few seconds before he relents and returns my smile, jerking me roughly to him to plant a hard kiss on my mouth. "You and that damn smile…"

He bends his head and nips the skin of my neck, sending a shower of chills raining down my chest and shoulders.

"Did you say we needed to leave this room? Because if you keep this up, we won't be going anywhere," I tell him, warmth coiling in my stomach. No matter what else is going on, no matter how much drama and distress is swirling through our lives, we always have this. Always. A fire that can't be extinguished. A love that can't be quenched.

"Shit," I hear him grumble. He releases me again, just as reluctantly as he did a few minutes ago, and he looks down into my face. "Let's get this over with."

I take a deep breath, nod and hold on tight to his hand as he opens the door and pulls me out of our safe haven.

SIX

Cash

I FEEL protective of Olivia. I mean, I always do, but it's more pronounced now. Like, *right now.* At this moment, I feel the need to rescue her. From my past, from the people in it, from the uncertainties of the future.

Part of me wants to turn around, scoop her up and carry her as far away from here as I can get her. Only I can't do that. If Sophie is right, if this little girl is mine, I can't just abandon her. I can't just walk away. She's already been in this world and without a father for, what, nine years? I don't want to add even one more year to that number.

So here I go, walking into the stickiest of situations—trying to merge the past and the present, trying to integrate the woman from yesterday into my marriage of today.

I feel Olivia's fingers tighten around mine when we round the corner to find Sophie sitting about halfway down the bar, on a stool, slumped over like she's asleep.

I clear my throat and her head shoots up. When she locates us, her lips spread into a tentative smile. She gets up and stands beside the stool until we reach her. Her eyes are trained on Olivia.

"Do you mind if I say something first?" she asks, addressing my wife rather than me.

I glance down at Olivia. Her beautiful face is calm, not one bit of her inner turmoil showing through her creamy skin. "Of course not."

Always kind. Always polite. She's too good for me. But then again, I always knew that.

I pull her closer to my side and wind my arm around her waist. A united front against...whatever. Against *whom*ever.

"I want to apologize for my horrible timing last night." Sophie's eyes fill with tears and her chin trembles. I frown. I wasn't expecting this. The Sophie I knew never apologized, never backed down, never cried. She was the bravest person I knew back then, which was saying a lot. I guess we've both changed. "I would never, *never* have done that had I known that Cash was married. I didn't think he was the marrying type, but I guess...

We all change. Eventually. And I want you to know that I'm not here to cause trouble. I just want my little girl to know her father. That's all."

Olivia says nothing, just keeps smiling. I, however, feel no such need to hold my tongue. "Why now? Why the hell didn't you come to me when you knew you were pregnant?"

"I...I knew you wouldn't believe me. And my father...well, you know how he was."

"Was?"

She nods. "He died in April."

"I'm sorry to hear that."

"Yeah, Isabella and I are pretty much all each other has now. Your mom was the mother I never had and I heard she..."

"Yeah, right after you left."

"God, I hate I didn't get to see her again. To make things right. She was so good to me."

"She loved you like a daughter. It broke her heart when you left."

"If I could go back...do things differently..." She stares up into my eyes for several long seconds, enough for me to see that she came here wanting more than just to introduce her daughter to me. She came here *for me*, too.

"Things worked out for the best," I say, smiling as I look down at Olivia, brushing my lips across her forehead. She leans into me like she might fall over if I weren't right beside her. I feel another surge of anger toward Sophie for doing this to us, to *her*. Olivia doesn't deserve this. She deserves only happiness. And I know that none of this will make her happy.

"I, uh, I knew you'd want to know. About Isabella, I mean."

"Yeah. It would've been nice to know before now, though. I've missed half her damn childhood. What the hell were you thinking, Soph?" I ask, rising temper causing my voice to rise.

"I was trying to make a life for myself in Canada. Dad would hardly speak to me for months. I dropped out of school. I was a kid having a kid. You can't blame me for being stupid."

"But why now? Why after all this time?"

"I…we…we need a new start. After Dad…this was the only place that felt like home after he died. I thought…I remembered the club. And I knew about Greg…that you were running it now… I thought if you'd let me work a few shifts, just until I can get us settled, you could get to know your daughter. Decide whether you want us around or not."

Olivia stiffens beside me.

"Sophie, I don't think that's a good idea."

38

She bursts into tears. "I-I-I was af-fraid you'd say that. It's just that...we don't have anywhere else to go. I have no m-money, no j-job. And I don't know how I'm supposed to take care of Isabella until I find something. I just...I just..." She covers her face with her hands and bawls while Olivia and I just stand here watching her.

I feel my wife twitch once, twice and then, woman that she is, she steps forward to put her hand on Sophie's shaking shoulder. As if that was all the opening she needed, Sophie turns and throws her arms around Olivia and clings to her.

My eyes meet Olivia's over Sophie's head. In them is a mixture of helplessness, sympathy and a hollow sadness that makes my chest tight. She's the bigger person, the *better* person. That just makes me worry about her all the more. If Sophie is still the same woman I knew all those years ago, even deep down, this could spell trouble. But what Sophie doesn't realize is that I'm still enough the same man that if she backs me into a corner or hurts Olivia in any way, she won't like what happens next.

SEVEN

Olivia

I WANT to believe that this woman is sincere. I want to believe that her motives are simple and pure, and that she only wants her child to know her father. Since babies and motherhood have been at the forefront of my mind for a while now, I can understand that completely. It pains me to think of my own child being in that situation—homeless, fatherless, without the roots and ties of family. I'd have been lost without my father. He saved me from the influence of my mother, from the life that she'd have had me to live. I can't help wondering if this little girl needs saving from hers, too. As much as I'd like to believe she selflessly wants what's best for her child, the resentful parts of me are doubtful.

When she finally stops crying and pulls away, I'm grateful. I'm feeling weak and emotional myself and she's only making it worse. I mean, I was drawn to give her comfort, but I wasn't expecting…this, and I'm not entirely comfortable with it. I don't know this woman yet. And I'm still not sure I want to.

The thing is, I don't think I have a choice. At least not a good one. Not one that wouldn't put me at odds with my husband, and I would never do anything to push him away. Even if it means letting his ex and their daughter into my life.

I swallow a lump of emotion and take a step away from her. Her blue eyes are red-rimmed and swollen, and she looks like she hasn't slept in days.

"I'm sorry. I'm sure that's the last thing you wanted or needed this morning." I try my smile again. It's tremulous at best, but it seems to suffice as an answer. "I'm just… stressed. It's been a long couple of weeks and I haven't had a good night's sleep since…I can't even remember when."

"Have you been sleeping in your car?" Cash asks, a razor edge to his tone.

Sophie has the good grace to blush. "We stayed in a motel a few nights, but Izzy has really bad allergies and I think the industrial cleaners they use bother her. She does much better in a car if she can't be in a home."

A terrible sinking sensation spreads through the pit of my stomach. It's like a vacuum, threatening to suck me into the black hole developing at my center. My knees feel weak with it. My heart feels heavy with it.

I know where this is going and I feel powerless to stop it. This woman could be the mother of Cash's child. The little girl in the office could be Cash's daughter. How can I be the person to stand in the way of him helping them as much as possible? How can I be the person who is so insecure in her relationship with him that she demands he turn away his own flesh and blood simply because they make *me* uncomfortable? How can I be that woman?

I can't.

I just can't.

No matter how much I don't like it, no matter how much I wish Cash will turn out *not* to be the father, I can't be the one who drives a wedge between them. One day he would resent me for it. *I* would resent me for it. I don't want to be petty and heartless. I don't want to be needy and weak. I want to be strong, confident in Cash's love. Able to stand beside, come what may. Even if that is an old love with a new child.

So I take the bold step. I take control. At least I'll have that.

"You could stay at the condo," I blurt.

In my peripheral vision, I see Cash's head whip toward me. Whether in surprise or disapproval, I don't know. I'm not looking at him. I'm looking at Sophie.

"I couldn't do that. Besides, I wouldn't want to leave Isabella there unattended while I try to find a job. And then while I have to work. If only it were closer…"

"What is it that you want, Sophie?" Cash asks, crossing his thick arms over his thicker chest. I sneak a glance at him and he doesn't look very happy. "I'm not into games anymore."

Sophie's eyes dart from Cash to me and back again before she answers. Although her voice is meek when she speaks, something about her posture tells me that she's got a backbone of steel under there. And if she does, how has she allowed herself to get into this position? To what end?

I might never know, but it certainly looks like I'm going to have plenty of time to try and figure it out. My fear, the one that has my stomach sinking all over again, is playing out in real life. I can feel it before she even opens her mouth. And when she does, my heart burns in my chest.

"Honestly, I was hoping that you'd let me pick up some shifts here and stay in the back until I can find something else for Isabella and me. Just for a few weeks."

"That's out —"

She interrupts Cash before he can even finish his thought, finish what sounded like a denial of her request. "I'd know she was safe and I'd never be far. And you, you'd be able to get to know your daughter with her right here. We'd be so close. It would be perfect, Cash. Can't you see that?"

She tips her head to the side and takes a step toward him. It's my gasp—the gasp triggered by my imagination filling in all the blanks she's leaving open—that stops her. I see her sidelong glance in my direction and, for the first time since she walked into the club last night, I get a glimpse of what she wants. What she *really* wants.

And it's not just a bed and a job.

No, she wants much more than that. And I'm the only thing standing in her way.

EIGHT

Olivia

SOPHIE IS smart. I'll give her that.   She obviously knows Cash well enough to know that he can't be bulldozed or coerced. At least not without a damned effective weapon.

And a child–*his child*—is just such a weapon.

"I'm not asking you to do it for *me,* Cash. I'm asking you to do it for your daughter. So she can rest well. So she can know her father. At least until we can figure out a way forward."

"She'd have known her father already if you'd bothered to tell him that he had a daughter," he snaps testily.

Sophie casts her eyes down. "I know I should've told you sooner. I won't try to make excuses. But Cash, I was just a kid. And the way things ended between us...I just wasn't sure you'd welcome the news. I know I hurt you. I hurt you bad and…I can't tell you how much I regret that, but don't hold *my* mistakes against Izzy. She's just a little girl."

"Like I would do that. What kind of man do you think I am?" he growls angrily.

"I know what kind of man you *used to be*. I knew time and life and distance couldn't change you *that much*. You're too stubborn. Always have been." There's an intimate ring to her words and she smiles at him in a way that *I know* is meant to drag him back into yesteryear, when they were a couple. "That's why I knew I could bring her here. That you'd help. That you'd do right by your flesh and blood."

Cash surprises me by his next statement, by the blatant insinuation. But then again, he's never been one to pull punches.

"I'll always do right by my flesh and blood. As long as they *are* my flesh and blood."

Sophie manages to look offended, although something tells me she's not. Not really. If she knows Cash as well as she says she does, she'd know that he would want a paternity test. Cash and I haven't talked about it, but *I* had no doubts he'd want one. Any man with a brain would. And Cash has lots of brains. Anyone who is fooled by his muscles is just that—fooled.

46

"You think I'd lie about something like that?"

"I don't *think* anything, Sophie, but I want to know for sure. Surely you had to expect me to ask for proof."

"Look at her!" she cries in outrage, pointing toward the office where her daughter sleeps. "How could you deny it?"

"She looks just like you. How could I *not* question it?"

"Yes, she looks like me, only with *your* eyes."

"Only with *dark brown* eyes. Davenports don't hold the monopoly on that color. Surely that's not how you expected to convince me."

Cash's icy tone cools Sophie's indignation. "No, you're right. Lots of people have dark brown eyes. Eyes so dark they're almost black." She adds the last with heavy sarcasm. "And *of course* we'll submit to testing. Just as soon as the holidays are over and everything opens back up." Her voice softens and her expression turns to one of feminine sway. She's all but batting her eyelashes at him. "That's okay, isn't it? To wait until after the holidays? Surely you wouldn't make us leave right after Christmas just because the rest of the world closes their offices, would you?"

I could throw up all over her.

Cash's full lips thin into a tight, straight line. "Of course not. Don't be ridiculous."

At that, she smiles. "Yeah, that is kind of ridiculous, isn't it?"

Cash doesn't return her smile and I can do little more than just stand here and try not to baulk. I think I've had more than enough of this woman for the moment.

I clear my throat. "Well, if you'll be staying in the apartment here, I guess I'd better get our things together, right, babe?" I ask, smiling up at Cash, trying to act natural. Like my chest doesn't feel as though it's been ripped open by a dull knife.

"I'm coming. I'll help," he says, reaching out to brush his thumb over my cheekbone and give me that lopsided grin of his that I love so much.

"Olivia," Sophie says, forcing my eyes back to her and (purposely, no doubt) shattering the tiny moment Cash and I were sharing. I can't help wondering if that will be her role from here on out—disrupt at every opportunity. I turn my attention back to her, although it's considerably cooler now that I'm onto her ploy. Or at least I think I am.

"Yes?"

"Thank you. Truly. As one mother to another, I know you know how much this means to me." Ice forms across the surface of my heart and I can feel the color leave my face. "You *do* have children, right?"

"No. I-I don't have any children. Yet." I say the last emphatically, as if it's not even in question. I hope she can't detect the fear, the uncertainty, the *panic* in my heart that there's a distinct possibility that I won't be able to give my husband a child of our own.

"Oh. I just assumed…I mean, Cash wasn't really the marrying type, so I assumed you were…that he had to…"

Silence falls into the room like a thick, dark cloud until Cash's voice pierces it like an ominous crack of thunder.

"You assumed that she trapped me? That she tricked me into marrying her?"

Sophie's eyes widen. Obviously she *does* know Cash well enough to know when she's pushed him too far.

"No, I didn't mean it like that. I just meant that…I know how you used to be and…and…"

"I married Olivia because I can't live without her. I *wasn't* the marrying type until I met her. Now, I'm happier than I've ever been. *Ever.* And we *will* be having kids. We've got all the time in the world, though, so we're waiting until our house finished. Waiting until everything is perfect. As perfect as she is," he says, turning to smile down into my face and coming to my rescue in the most amazing way possible.

I lean up to place a quick kiss on his chin before I turn to walk away.

"Thank you, Olivia. And I'm sorry," Sophie calls out behind me.

My step stutters slightly. I want to turn around and snarl at her, to sneer that *I'm* sorry, too. Sorry that Cash ever knew her. Sorry that she found us. Sorry that he might've had a child with another woman. But I don't do any of that. I pull myself together and throw my brightest smile over my shoulder. "I just hope you know how to bartend."

And, with that, I leave her behind.

At least for the moment.

NINE

Cash

WHEN I find Olivia, she is standing in the doorway of the office, staring at the sleeping girl on the couch. I stop behind her, wrapping my arms around her and pulling her into my chest. She doesn't turn, but rests her head against my shoulder and continues staring at Isabella.

"I don't like that she calls her Izzy," she says in a whisper.

I smile. "I don't either. She doesn't look like an Izzy. She looks like an Isabella."

"Exactly," she agrees. After a full two minutes of silence, she speaks again. "She really is a beautiful child."

I don't argue with her because I can't. Isabella *is* a beautiful child. But what I *do* tell my wife is the truth as I see it. "No human will be as beautiful as *our* child will be, though. Her dazzling green eyes will confound scientists. Her creamy skin will entrance artists. And her brilliant smile will be the envy of the stars."

"God I love the way your mind works," she replies, a hitch in her voice.

I release her only enough to turn her toward me. Her emerald eyes are shiny with unshed tears. "I'm right, you know. There will be no comparison to what we create together."

She nods, but doesn't speak for a few seconds. "But still, she's beautiful," she says, tipping her head back toward Isabella. "And you'll love her, too. Because that's just who you are."

Even though her heart is breaking right inside her eyes, she's trying to make the best of this. To think the best of *me*. It makes me love her that much more.

"I'm the best me when I'm with you. I'm the best me *because* of you."

As I watch, fear skates in across Olivia's features, draining all the color from her face. "Cash, I'm scared."

I pull her hard against me, burying my nose in her neck and bending to lift her off her feet. "Don't be scared. You've got me. All of me. You had me from the second you took my shirt off. You stripped me that night. More than you'll ever know. No one could ever take me away from you, or from the family we're going to have. No one. I swear it."

I feel the shudder that trembles through her slight body and I squeeze her tighter, wishing I could absorb her hurt. Take it away. Make all of this better. Because it seems to be getting worse. Now not only do I possibly have a daughter, but my ex is staying in my apartment and working in my bar. With my wife. And while Sophie always had a good heart, she's devious and determined. If she thinks she can get me back, she won't think twice about doing whatever she thinks she needs to in order to get Olivia out of the way. That's why I'm going to have to set her straight as soon as I can get her alone. And keep an eye out for anything suspicious. I still care about Sophie, but I can't say I'm glad to see her again. She was trouble before. I get the feeling she's gotten even worse with age.

But still, she is an old friend. An old *family* friend. And my mom loved her. And more than any of that, she might be the mother of my first child. The results of that paternity test will set us on a path forward. Until then...I just have to bide my time.

"I love you," Olivia mumbles as she turns her face toward my ear.

My favorite words.

"I love you more," I tell her.

"Not. Possible."

"Quite. Possible."

"Never."

"Always."

I feel her lips spread against my skin and I know she's smiling. That's become sort of our thing.

"I think we've got some...work to do tonight, don't you?"

"I think you might be right. How about we light up the Christmas tree at the condo? The *right* way?"

"Mmmm," I growl against her throat, my dick twitching at the imagery. "You, naked, bathed in twinkling lights, moaning my name? Hell yeah! That really *is* the right way!"

TEN

Olivia

I HAVE just finished packing the last of our things and stripping the sheets from the bed when my phone rings. I answer it, tucking my cell between my shoulder and my ear as I take the sheets to the washing machine and stuff them inside. "Hello?"

"May I speak with Olivia Davenport please?"

"This is she."

"Yes, ma'am, I'm calling from St. Joseph's Hospital. You're the emergency contact listed for Darrin Townsend. Do you know someone by that name?"

My heart begins to pound wildly as my hands still on the closed lid of the washer. "Yes, he's my father. Is something wrong?"

"We have your father here in the cardiac cath lab. He was transferred from an urgent care unit in Salt Springs. Would you mind coming to the registration area to fill out some paperwork?"

I am instantly sick with worry. My father is in the hospital? In a cath lab? Does this mean he had a heart attack?

Ohgod ohgod ohgod!

"Of course. I'll be there as soon as I can get there. I'm leaving now."

"Thank you. When you're finished at registration, you can come back to the cath lab waiting room and call the nurse's desk from the phone in there. Just ask for Amber and I'll update you."

"Okay. I-I will. Thank you."

"You're welcome. See you soon."

"Yes. Thanks."

My fingers are trembling when I press the END button on my phone. As I was packing up our things to take to the condo, I made the mistake of thinking to myself that nothing could make this holiday worse.

But I was wrong.

So, so wrong.

I abandon the sheets and the packing and go straight for my shoes and purse. I walk out into the garage bay to where my husband is loading the car with our stuff. He looks up from behind the trunk lid when I call his name. His expression falls into one of deep concern when he sees my face.

"What is it? What's wrong?"

He knows me so well.

Cash doesn't hesitate to stop what he's doing and take the few steps to me. He winds his long fingers around my upper arms and bends to look into my eyes, his own nearly-black ones glittering with apprehension.

"It's Dad. He-he's in the hospital. The cath lab. At St. Joseph's. I have to go fill out paperwork. I...I...I don't know what's going on, but it must be bad, Cash. It must be *really* bad."

I feel tight as a drum from head to toe. Rigid, like my muscles are bracing themselves. For what, I'm not sure.

Gently, my husband takes the keys from the edge of my purse and ushers me to the passenger side of the car, opening the door and shuffling me inside. I stare straight ahead, my mind buzzing around a dozen different scenarios, kind of like buzzards circling the air over a fresh kill. Watching. Waiting.

When Cash slides in behind the wheel and starts the engine, he hits the button to lift the garage door and then takes my fingers in his. They're warm and firm and familiar. Safe. "Whatever it is that's going on, he'll come through. Your dad is one tough man. Remember when he broke his leg? How hard it was to get him to stay down? He's a fighter. Strong. Stubborn. Just like his daughter."

"I know he is, but stubborn can't stop a heart attack."

"No, but it can bring him through it. He'd do anything for you, to keep you happy and never hurt you. He knows he can't leave you yet. That's why he'll fight tooth and nail—*for you*. You know that."

"Yeah, I know. But Cash, his heart? Oh God!"

I drop my face into my hand and will myself not to fall apart. I want to. I feel like I need to in some ways. Like the stress of the last couple of days is just too much and I need to check out of reality for a little while. But I can't. Now is not the time to be weak and frail. Now is the time to suck it up and be strong. Even though I don't feel strong.

Cash brushes his lips over the knuckles of my left hand before releasing it to back out of the garage. I feel the loss immediately. When he's touching me, I feel as though nothing can hurt me. But the instant he lets go...

Always sensitive to my needs, to what I'm thinking and feeling, Cash reaches for my hand again after he pulls out onto the main road. He doesn't let it go until we pull into St. Joseph's parking lot some thirty minutes later.

ELEVEN

Cash

I DIAL Gavin's number. He answers on the second ring. "Did I wake you?" I ask when I hear his sleepy voice.

"No. Just, er, lazing in bed."

"Am I *interrupting?*"

Gavin's laugh says it all. "Nothing that won't be resumed the instant I hang up."

"Make it quick, Thor," Ginger chimes in loudly from the background. "I was right in the middle of showing Gavin a neat trick."

I can't help smiling. Not only am I happy for Gavin and Ginger, Olivia will be thrilled. And she could use some thrilling news.

"Does this trick involve clothing?" I ask, teasing.

"Not at present," Gavin replies distractedly.

"I'll be quick then. I need you to do me a favor."

"Anything."

"Olivia's dad is in the hospital. She's back there in the waiting room now. They let her see him before he went in for a heart catheterization. Looks like he's had a heart attack."

"Oh shit, mate! I'm sorry. Give Olivia our love."

I hear Ginger asking him questions in a softer voice, one that's laced with concern. I pause while Gavin answers her before I continue.

"Listen, I just came out to call Nash so that he could tell Marissa's dad. I had a message that Stella can't work tonight. Obviously Olivia can't fill in for her and I think everyone else pretty much had plans. Sophie will be working at Dual for a few weeks. Think you could show her the ropes tonight?"

"Sure," he says in his congenial Australian way. "Does she have any bartending experience?"

"I don't know. We didn't really get that far, but we're in a pinch, so..."

"Well, it just so happens that I might know someone who's a very experienced...bartender, who might be willing to help out. If I ask nicely. Very nicely."

I roll my eyes. I really don't need to hear Gavin when he's half talking to a nude Ginger in bed. "Whatever, man, just work it out, okay?"

"Consider it worked out."

"I don't expect to be around for a while, but I've got my phone if you need me."

"No worries. Focus on that beautiful wife of yours. I'll take care of everything else."

"Thanks, man."

"Later," he says and then the line goes dead. I try not to think about what's probably already happening between those two. Ginger has become almost like a sister. I prefer not to think of her in *any* kind of sexual manner, much less naked, possibly riding my best friend first thing in the morning.

I shudder at the mere suggestion.

Quickly, I dial Nash's number, trying to put all images of Ginger and Gavin out of my mind. He answers on the first ring.

"Need me to smuggle you out of the country until Sophie leaves?" he asks as soon as he picks up, his voice smug. He always did like to rub it in when I got into trouble.

Asshole.

"I haven't needed bailing out of trouble in years. Now you on the other hand…"

"Not anymore," he defends. "In a few months, I'll be a father. I can't be getting into trouble any more. From here on it's the straight and narrow."

"Well, my trouble isn't of the Sophie variety. At least not right this minute. I'm at the hospital with Olivia."

Before I can explain, Nash interrupts. "What? What's wrong? What happened? Is she okay?"

"It's not her. It's her dad. Darrin had a heart attack. He's having a heart cath right now. Hopefully they'll be able to put in a stent, but they said if it's bad…"

"If it's bad what?"

"If it's bad, he could end up having open heart surgery."

"Oh shit!"

"Yeah. I know. We're hoping for the best, but… Even though those two are the way they are, Olivia wanted her uncle to know, so I told her I'd take care of it. So now *you* can take care of it."

"I like how that works. Putting it off on your brother. Nice."

"I thought so."

"I'm sure you did," he replies sardonically, but I know he's just playing. He knows I'd do anything for Olivia because he's the same way over his wife.

"How's the, uh, pregnancy, by the way?"

"She's sick as hell until about ten in the morning and then she's fine. Doing great. And I gotta tell ya, bro," Nash says, dropping his voice low, "I'm loving the hell out of what's happening to her body. You'll see what I mean when Olivia gets pregnant. Her boobs...damn! She's got the tits of a porn star. And horny! Holy shit is she horny! Now I see why people have an ass-ton of kids. This part's a lot more fun than what I expected."

"Dude! That's some shit I did *not* need to hear," I tell him in mock horror. In truth, though, it makes me a little sad to think that Olivia and I might not be able to *ever* experience all that together. I'd never let her know that it bothers me or that I'd miss it if I couldn't see her belly grow round with my baby. It would hurt her even more than what she's already hurting. But I *do* think about it. I probably mourn it as much as Olivia does, but I hide it. Because I love her. I love her more than I need to share my own feelings on the matter. And I love her more than a missed pregnancy or pre-baby tits. She's all that matters to me. Plain and simple.

Nash laughs. "I love listening to you squirm."

"You're one sick bastard."

"So I hear," he says, sobering a little. "Want me to tell Dad, too?"

"Yeah, if you would. I'll get word out to everyone when he's in a room or…whatever."

"Sounds good. Anything you need? Anything we can do?"

"Nah. Gavin's holding down the fort at Dual. He can keep an eye on Sophie. Anything else can wait until Darrin's out of the woods because I'm not leaving Olivia until we know he's okay."

"Don't blame you, Cash. Call if you need me, though."

"Thanks. Later, man."

"See ya."

When the line goes dead, I let my arm drop to my side and I think about where we are, what's happened and what's likely *to* happen. The convergence of all this shit, this perfect storm of shit, on my wife worries me. She was struggling with not being able to get pregnant anyway. Now her cousin is expecting and my ex showed up with a child that could well be mine. On top of that, her father just had a heart attack. Who knows how that could end up?

Olivia is strong. One of the strongest people I've ever met, but I'm not sure how she's going to hold up under all this if it gets much worse.

As though my thoughts summoned her—and another pile of shit to add to the storm—Olivia comes rushing out the door, face pale, eyes watering.

"They're taking him into surgery, Cash! They're taking Dad in for open heart surgery. They said he just had a massive heart attack in the room back there. The blockage is so severe they can't put in a stent. They said something about a widow-maker. Cash, they don't know if he's going to make it. My dad might die. He might die!"

With eyes as big and shiny as the full moon on a clear summer night, she gulps in air once, twice, and then crumbles right in my arms.

I didn't know how much worse things could get. I guess I just got my answer.

Until my phone bleeps with an incoming text.

From Sophie.

How the hell did she get my number?

TWELVE

Olivia

"WHO IS it?" I manage to ask when Cash checks his phone and slides it quickly back into his pocket.

He shrugs, pressing his lips to my forehead. "Work. Nothing important."

A knife of unease slices through me, but almost immediately my current worries rush in to overtake all other thought. My father—the man who raised me, the man who shielded me from my mother, the man who bandaged my scraped knees and watched cartoons with me when I was sick—is going into one of the most major surgeries a human being can have. They're going to put him to sleep and cut his chest wide open. They're going to re-route the circulation of his heart and breathe for him. They're going to replace vital arteries and hope that they hold. Then they're going to sew him back up and pray that he wakes up when it's over. And if one thing goes wrong, if there's one glitch in that intricate process, I could lose him. I could never see his smile, hear his voice or feel his hug again for the rest of my life. And neither will my children. They'll never know the amazing man their grandfather is.

I'm gripped by a fear so poignant, a panic so overwhelming that my pulse speeds. It races so fast that my head swims and my stomach sloshes.

"Listen to me," Cash whispers against my hair, halting the tailspin I was falling into. "Darrin Townsend is *not* going down this way. That crazy son of a bitch is gonna come out laughing. You know how he is. He'd kick the ass of anyone or anything that tried to get between him and his daughter. Surgery included."

I let out a shaky breath. My father *is* strong. And he *does* love me. I know he'd do anything within his power to keep me from pain and harm. But this...

"I know, but this is serious. So serious."

"It is. But so is he when he means business. Think about how he stays up all night worrying about his sheep. Think about how hard he fights to keep every single one healthy, alive and accounted for. He's a determined man, especially when it comes to what he loves. And *you,* he loves most of all. He'll pull through, baby. If for no other reason, he'll do it for you. God gave him a backbone of steel and probably a heart just as strong. Have faith in that."

I turn my face to the side and press my ear to Cash's chest. I can hear the steady thud of his heart and I close my eyes to focus on it. So comforting. So reassuring. So strong. Like my father's. I've heard it pressed to my ear in much this same way for my whole life when he'd hold me. Just because his vessels are sick doesn't mean his heart is. They caught it in time. He couldn't have been in a better place for this to happen. And now they're going to fix him. Then he'll come back to me. To share his smile, to hold his grandkids, to grow old right before my eyes.

Have faith.

As calm begins to ripple through me, my focus spreads out to include other things, other people.

"Our things…I left without finishing. I need to get that stuff to the condo so Sophie can have a place to stay."

"I'll take care of it. Don't worry about that right now."

"I would go back, but I don't know what to expect from the next few hours. Or the next few days for that matter. I don't want to leave just yet."

"I've got it, baby. This is where your focus needs to be. It's more important. Leave the rest to me."

I pause, nibbling my lip in indecision. "Cash?"

"Hmmm?" he murmurs, his hand stroking my hair in that way he does that makes me feel like the most adored and cherished person in the history of the world.

I almost hate to bring this up, but I'm so emotional right now it seems to be beyond my self-control *not* to ask.

"Sophie said she hurt you. Did she?"

I feel as much as hear his sigh. "At the time she did."

I close my eyes. I had hoped he would say that she didn't, that she was just being dramatic. Or arrogant. Or clueless. I was hoping that he never really cared about her very much. Only it seems that he did. At least for a time.

"Wh-what happened between you two?"

"Olivia, I know all this with your dad has turned you inside out, but don't let it cast a shadow of doubt on things you *know* to be true. Like the fact that I love you and *only you*. Like the fact that

70

nothing and no one will ever come between us. Like the fact that you're the most important person in my life. Period. Sophie is a girl from my past. Nothing more. If you couldn't reach out and touch her, I'd tell you she was a ghost. There's not even enough there for you to sink your teeth into. Please, please, *please* don't let her get to you."

"That's easier said than done," I reply quietly, my heart aching all over again.

"Then when it gets hard to do, come to me. I'll set you straight. I'll tell you who comes first. And second. And third." He leans back, forcing me away from his chest so that he can peer down into my face. "It's you. And it always will be. No matter who comes rolling through our door, you'll always be the one who matters most. Got it?"

I do my best to grin. "Got it."

He brushes his lips over mine and then urges my head back onto his chest. When his phone bleeps again from his pocket, I don't ask why he doesn't check it. I just remind myself of his words. And try my best not to worry about ghosts.

THIRTEEN

Cash

WHEN OLIVIA takes a call from her father's neighbor, I reach into my pocket for my phone. Two texts from an unknown number, but the first line of the first text tells me who the number belongs to.

Cash, it's Sophie.

I don't bother reading the rest of the message or the next one until I've angrily tapped out a single question.

Me: How did you get this number?

Within seconds, I see the three little bubbles pop up, an indication that she's typing a response. I read her other text as I wait. She's asking if everything is okay and saying that our things are still there. Before I can reply, her answer to my question displays on the screen.

Sophie: The business cards on your desk. I saw them when I went in to wake Izzy.

Her answer diffuses some of my irritation. I'd forgotten about those.

Me: Oh. Right.

Sophie: Well?

Me: Well what?

Sophie: Is everything okay?

I toy with how to respond. For some reason, telling Sophie too much feels like a betrayal to Olivia, even though she could find out from any number of other people. It's not like it's a big secret.

Me: Olivia's father is having surgery, I respond vaguely.

Sophie: I hope he's okay. If there's anything I can do, just ask.

Me: Nothing you can do.

Sophie: I'm going to fill in at the club tonight. Don't worry about a thing. I've tended bar before.

Me: But not at *my bar*.

Sophie: No, but I'm a quick learner. Remember?

She adds a winking smiley face to the end of the sentence. It makes the question seem flirtatious. Suggestive. Unfortunately, I know exactly what she means by that. It's a reference to a conversation we had many years ago when I took her virginity. She asked me to show her how to please me. So I did. Not long after that, during a particularly…heated night at her house when her parents were gone, she teased me after sex, saying that she was a quick learner. At the time, it was good sex, but I was a kid. What the hell did I know about good sex?

I don't rise to her bait. If she thinks that there's a chance for us to get back together, I mean to put an end to that little spark of hope right off the bat.

Me: No. But I hope you're right. I don't have time to babysit you.

Sophie: You won't have to babysit me. I'll be running that bar like a pro in a couple of weeks.

Me: All you need to do is keep the customers happy.

Sophie: I'm good at pleasing people.

Another suggestive remark? Or am I making too much of everything she says? Am I *looking* for something that's not there? Am I looking for something to be pissed about?

I scrub a hand over my face. What a damn nightmare! Of all the things Olivia and I need in our life right now, none of this comes anywhere close. The arrival of an ex, a child that could be mine, being uprooted during the holidays, Olivia's father having surgery—our life and our plans will be taking a back seat for the moment. Indefinitely. And that makes me uneasy as hell.

FOURTEEN

Olivia

I HAVE the strangest feeling that Cash is hiding something from me when I walk back into the little waiting room. His expression is unusually tense. Even the smile he gives me looks…uneasy.

"Everything okay?" he asks, reaching out to stroke my upper arms when I stop in front of him.

"Yeah. That was Arnie. Just checking on Dad. Word spreads fast in small towns."

"That it does," he replies noncommittally. "Hey, you getting hungry?"

I glance at the clock on the wall. It's after lunch, but I don't feel the least bit hungry. Just uptight. Worried. Downright afraid, even.

"Not really, but you should go get you something."

He shakes his head. "Nope. I don't want to leave you."

"You can't stand here and starve just because I'm not hungry."

"I can and I will."

As if to speak up in dissent, Cash's stomach growls loudly.

"I think your body would beg to differ."

"I only listen to that thing when it's hungry for *you*, which is all the time. In all other areas, I can control myself."

I can't help smiling. "Lucky for you, that's the one area I *want you* out of control."

"Then you should be very happy. I can just *think* about you without clothes and...*damn!*" he growls, his eyes glistening black.

Although I'm happy that he still reacts to me that way after all this time, I'm too distracted and burdened to feel like doing anything about it.

"Well, since there's nothing that can be done about *that* hunger, at least go take care of the other one. You might have to be strong for both of us and you can't very well do that when you're starving."

"I could be strong for you on my deathbed."

"Let's not test that for another sixty or seventy years, k? Now go eat. There's time while he's still in surgery. Besides, I've got some calls to make. Someone is going to have to take care of the farm for a while."

"Baby, just tell me what to do, who to call and I'll do it."

"It's okay. I know these people. It's just better for me to do it. Take care of the things you need to now, before he gets out."

"Are you sure? I hate leaving you here alone."

"It's fine. I promise. You're just making sure that you can be here for me the rest of the night. That's all. Besides, I've got things to do. So do you. Just be back in a couple of hours. They said it would take four to six hours, so you've got time."

"I guess I probably need to get our things then. In case I can't get back over there tonight." He seems hesitant to bring it up.

I swallow hard. Back to Sophie. "Okay. Now's as good a time as any, I suppose."

"You know you can always change your mind. We can figure out something else."

It's tempting. So, so tempting. The curve of my lips feels tight. Forced. Fake. "No, it's fine. It's not permanent. And the little girl shouldn't have to suffer because of her mother's poor decision making."

Cash cups my face in his big hands. "You're the most amazing woman I've ever had the pleasure of knowing."

"And don't you forget it," I tease.

"I could never forget you. You've got the ass of a sixteen-year-old Russian gymnast."

"Nice," I laugh, lightly slapping his arm. "How very...specific."

"All your body parts are world-class. Any time you want specifics, I'm happy to share."

"Maybe later."

He bends his head to kiss my neck. "Promise?"

"Promise."

"Then I'll hurry back."

"Please do."

When he pulls away, digging his car keys out of his pocket, I want to jerk him back to me, to hold on tight and not let him out of my sight. But I can't do that. Healthy adults in a healthy relationship don't do that to one another. No matter how much they want to. Or how afraid they are.

"Text me if you need anything. I'll bring it as I come."

"Just you."

"That's a given," he says, winking at me before he turns and heads for the door. "Be back soon."

"Be careful."

"I will. Love you." He says the last as he's disappearing around the corner.

"Cash!" I call.

He pops his head back into view. "Babe?"

"I love you, too."

He eyes me for a second and then walks back to me. As if he knows exactly what I need, he takes me in his arms and lifts me off the floor. When my face is level with his, he professes earnestly, "I love you more."

"Not. Possible."

"Quite. Possible."

"Never."

"Always."

After a deep yet sweet kiss, he sets me on my feet and makes his way out of the room. I stand watching the doorway long after he's gone.

FIFTEEN

Cash

I KNOW Gavin's on top of things, but in this particular instance, I'm not quite comfortable leaving him to deal with Sophie. At least not yet. I know what she's capable of—or at least what she *was* capable of when I knew her a lifetime ago—and I don't want her left to her own devices, unchecked. He needs to know what she's like and what her background is. He needs to know where I stand on everything so that there's no misunderstanding. For anybody.

When I pull back into the garage at the apartment behind Dual, I walk around front and go in the main doors rather than entering through the apartment. Already it doesn't feel like my home anymore and I don't like the feeling. It's where Olivia and I have spent countless happy nights and I'm not overly fond of having someone else sleep there.

The bar is empty when I walk in, so I head to the office. Gavin is behind the desk filling out paperwork when I stop in the doorway.

He raises his head and gives me a nod of acknowledgement before returning his attention to his task.

"How's Olivia holding up?" he asks in his Australian lilt.

"She's...holding."

"And how are *you* holding up?" Something in his voice is knowing. He has obviously deduced that my existence is on the verge of being dragged into a shitstorm of drama, and he knows me well enough to know that I hate drama. I think most men do.

"I haven't broken anything yet, so there's that."

He grins, but still doesn't look up. "I guess that's something. What's up?"

It annoys me that he's still so engrossed in what he's doing. I need his full attention right now. This is important. "What the hell are you doing?"

"Filling out the bloomin' ass ton of paperwork you have for your employees." He finally raises questioning eyes back to mine. "Unless you don't want me to do these for her."

I don't have to ask who "her" is. "No, I want them on file for her, too."

"Well damn," he says with a sigh, jotting something at the bottom of the last page and then turning them all back over to tap them into a neat pile. "That's not *at all* the answer I was hoping for." He says this with a grin as he leans back in the chair and laces his fingers behind his head.

"We need the protection," I explain.

"So it's like that."

"Yeah, it's like that."

Gavin leans forward, lowering his voice. "I don't trust her either."

"Why?" I ask, curious as to his answer.

Gavin is not only my friend and the manager of Dual, but he's the most cautious man I've ever met. No doubt it's a result of his time spent working as a mercenary. He's had to learn to be a good and quick judge of character, to be suspicious as a rule and cautious to a fault. That came in pretty damn handy during that mess with Olivia. I got to see his instincts in action. I had hoped never to need them again, but something about Sophie…I don't know. It just makes me uneasy. And now, knowing that Gavin doesn't trust her either…well, that only makes me *more* skeptical.

I guess I can only hope that whatever it is about her that's setting off red flags for both of us doesn't end up being anything that requires Gavin's particular brand of expertise.

He shrugs. "Nothing concrete yet. Just a feeling."

"Your feelings give *me* feelings," I tell him.

"That's because you're smart and I'm a damn good judge of character."

"That's just what I was thinking. But really, what is it that bothers you?"

"I can't put my finger on it, but I can do a bit of digging if that's all right with you."

I wonder for a second if I'm being neurotic in my paranoia, but then I think of my wife and I realize that I'm overprotective for good reason. I'd rather take the beating of a lifetime than to see her hurt. And if Sophie can hurt her in any way, even by hurting *me*, then I'm damn sure going to do everything I can to prevent it. And the only way I can do that is to keep my guard up and find out everything I can in the meantime.

"Fine by me. More than fine, actually. I need to know if there's anything…well, you know."

"Yeah, I know. In fact, I have an acquaintance I can call. Someone who's especially talented in the finding people. And in the finding out of things *about* those people."

"Any friend of yours is a friend of mine."

"I don't know as I'd call him a *friend* so much as an asset."

"Is he dangerous?"

"More than anyone I've met in a long time. But only to a certain…variety of people."

"And what 'variety' is that?"

"The variety that he goes looking for."

I hold my friend's blue eyes, reading between the lines and listening to what he's saying without saying anything at all. In the end, I trust Gavin. And if Gavin thinks it's safe to bring this guy on board, then so be it. He's done things for me and for Olivia that go above and beyond the duty of a friend. To say that I trust him with my life would be an understatement. The thing is, I trust him with Olivia's. And *that* is a bigger deal to me than trusting him with my own.

"If you think he can help, bring him in."

"I'll make the call. Might take him a few days anyway. That okay with you?"

I sigh. "I guess I've got nothing but time, man."

Gavin tips his head toward the closed apartment door behind him, the one from which I can hear cartoons playing loudly. "You think she's yours?"

"Hard to say. She *could* be and I guess that's enough to keep her around until I know for sure. I mean, if she is...I just can't turn my back on her. On either of them."

"No need to explain. I get it, mate. I just hope there's not more to this."

Gavin is voicing my concerns, which sort of validates them in my head. "Me, too, G. Me, too."

My gut is telling me—like Gavin's gut is telling him—that Sophie's up to something. And, dammit, I'm going to find out what it is. One way or the other.

"So did you come by just to see my pretty face? Or was there something else?"

"We left in a hurry, so I'm here to get our things. Olivia was finishing up packing when she got the call."

"Well, I don't think it bothered your new guest. She and her little girl are still back there, I guess. She'd mentioned going for something to eat, but I haven't seen her come out this way. And her car is still parked out front, so..."

I take a deep breath. "Did we have a Dual shirt for her? Or have you checked?"

"We had one. I ordered some extra for Olivia. Evidently they're the same size."

I feel like curling my lip. I don't know why that pisses me off, but it does. "Good. Keep an eye on her."

"Will do, mate. If she gets out of line, I'd say Ginger will be more than happy to bring her back in." His smile says he'd love to see a cat fight involving his feisty redhead.

"So, you're a thing now?"

His grin speaks volumes. "Wouldn't you like to know?"

"No. Not really. She's like a sister. Just the thought of…"

I shudder and Gavin laughs.

"Your loss, man. She's quite…I mean she's…she's… damn!"

I hold up my hand to make him stop. "I get the picture. You don't have to…"

That just seems to make him laugh that much harder.

"You'd better go get your shit before I start giving you details then."

He doesn't have to tell me twice.

I round the desk and knock on the door at the back of the office, the one that leads into my apartment. There's no response at first, but then the door eases open and a pair of sparkling black eyes peek up at me from the crack.

"Can I speak to your mom?" I ask, not knowing whether to ask her if I can come in or…

She nods and opens the door wider. When I step through, she turns away, calling out to her mother before resuming her place on the bed facing the television. "Momma!"

Within seconds, the bathroom door swings open and a freshly showered Sophie walks out. Her eyes round when she sees me and mine round when I see her. Hers in surprise; mine in anger.

She's wearing a shirt. Only a shirt. And the damn thing is *mine*.

SIXTEEN

Cash

"WHAT THE hell are you doing?" is what I want to ask. Or more like growl. The way it sounds in my head is nothing so nice as a polite "asking."

Sophie's familiarity, like we're still two high school kids who are banging in the back seat of my car every chance we get, annoys the shit out of me. She's up to something. I can feel it. I just don't have a damn clue what it is. And as much as I want to bark questions at her and demand that she take off my shirt, I don't. I'm too aware of the big brown eyes peeking up at me from Isabella's perch on the bed. When I glance at her, she looks quickly away, pretending to be absorbed in her cartoons again.

I turn back to Sophie.

"What are you doing here? How's Olivia's father?" she asks, raising her hands above her head to fluff her wet hair. She shakes and twists an inordinate amount, enough to make her hard nipples strain against the material of my shirt. I'm sure she's doing it on purpose.

"Can I talk to you for a minute?" I ask mildly, reaching for her upper arm and wheeling her around toward the bathroom before she can even answer me. I keep my calm until the door is shut, trapping us in the steamy room together. Keeping my voice low, I curl my fingers around Sophie's other arm and jerk her up against my chest. "Just what the hell do you think you're doing?"

I don't want the little girl to hear me, but I want Sophie to know just how much she's pissed me off. If she can't hear it in my voice, she can damn sure see it in my furious face, glaring at hers from less than a foot away.

"I...I needed a shower. I thought...I thought we were going to be staying here. And you'd be at the hospital all day. If I'd known you were coming back, I'd have waited. I'm sorry, I just..."

She actually looks bewildered, which cools my temper a little. Maybe I'm overreacting. She really *wouldn't have* known I was coming so soon. Maybe the shower thing was purely coincidental. But wearing my shirt...that's got to stop.

I release her arms and step back. "No, you can make yourself at home. For a while at least. But what's up with you wearing my clothes?"

She looks down at herself and then back up at me. "Oh, God! I know how this must look. I'm so sorry, Cash! I hadn't brought the rest of our luggage in yet and I didn't want to wake Izzy, so I just grabbed something from the closet and hopped in the shower. I assumed since it wasn't packed that it would be okay."

"Olivia was a little distracted when she left, as I'm sure you can imagine," I snap defensively.

"I'm sure. I mean…her father…Oh God! I guess I…I just assumed that maybe the remaining clothes were things you planned on donating to Goodwill or something. I'm really sorry. I'll wash it as soon as I get dressed and put it back where I found it. I just…I…" she stammers nervously. She tucks her chin and backs away from me, raising a hand to rub her fingers across her forehead. "Jesus, what a mess I'm making of things!"

Her voice is low and quiet. Laced with distress. I feel guilty for giving her such a hard time, for assuming the worst when the only reason I have to *believe* the worst is the old Sophie that I used to know. Maybe she *has* changed. I'll never know if

I don't stop accusing her of things before I even know she's guilty of them.

"Look, it's fine. Just a misunderstanding. In the future, though, don't wear anything that could be mine or Olivia's. That's just not...don't do that."

"You don't have to explain," she rushes in to say. "I totally get it. It would look awful if anyone else saw it. They might assume..." She sighs and shakes her head woefully. "I'm sorry, Cash. I never meant to...I just never meant to make trouble. If I'd known you were married, I wouldn't have come."

That irritates the shit out of me. "No? So you'd just have kept the existence of my daughter from me *forever*? Is that it?"

She raises her eyes to mine. They're wide, like a cornered animal. "No, I wouldn't do that. I mean...I'd have at least done things differently."

"Like how? Like telling me when Isabella was a baby rather than waiting until she was half grown?" I can't keep the bitter anger out of my voice.

"I should've told you. I realize that now. But please, Cash, just give me a second chance. I made mistakes. Lots of them. But I'm trying...*trying my damnedest* to do them better now. To do them right. Starting with making our daughter a part of your life. I'm sorry if my presence dredges up painful memories. I guess I was hoping we could put the past behind us."

Her eyes plead with me. They seem sincere.

Seem.

But I can't let my guard down. This *is* Sophie after all. Maybe she's changed. But then again, maybe she hasn't. Time will tell, but until it does, I'll be keeping my eye on her.

"Fine. Then let's leave the past in the past and focus on the little girl in the next room."

Her smile is tentative. "That's all I want."

I narrow my eyes on her, wishing I could see inside her head. Wishing I knew if she was telling the truth. "Is it?"

"Of course. What else would bring me here?"

That is the million dollar question.

SEVENTEEN

Olivia

DESPITE THE turmoil that permeates nearly every corner of my life right now, I'm overwhelmed by the strangest peace, one that assures me everything is going to be all right. It makes no sense really. I mean, my father is in surgery—crazy serious surgery—fighting for his life and my husband might have a daughter attached to a sneaky bitch from his past. I have no reason to think *anything* is going to be fine.

Yet I do.

When my phone rings, I don't even glance at the caller ID before I answer. "Hello?"

"How ya holdin' up, doll?" comes Ginger's voice.

"I'm okay. Pretty sure I'm going crazy, but otherwise I'm okay."

"Why do you say that?"

"Because I'm optimistic."

"That doesn't mean you're crazy. It just means you're naïve."

Even though she can't see it, I shrug. "Maybe they're the same thing. What do I know?"

"Sounds like you could use some company. Want me to come sit with you?"

"Only if you're going to give me gory details about you and Gavin. I'm tired of thinking about and talking about *my* problems."

"You're using the spillage of details as a means of blackmail? With *me*? It's like you don't know me at all."

At that, I smile. "Or do I?"

"Sneaky, sneaky," she clucks. "I like the cut of your jib, young lady. Give me a few minutes and I'll be there, ready to share things you'll probably never be able to forget. Consider yourself warned."

"You and your insane sexual escapades don't scare me."

"So you say *now*," she replies, adding a maniacal laugh before she hangs up.

I'm still shaking my head when she rounds the corner into the waiting room. She grins. I grin.

"What if I'd said I didn't want company?" I ask, sliding over on the small vinyl couch to make room for my friend.

She rolls her eyes and tucks her blonde hair behind one ear as she takes a seat beside me. "Like *that* would ever happen."

"Right? Because no one *ever* doesn't want *your* company."

"Exactly," she says, leaning back, satisfied. "So, why are you going crazy?"

My sigh is deep and long. "My perfect life is turning into a worse pile-up than that one on I-85 last week. Little by little, one by one, my cars are crashing."

Ginger's face melts into an expression of tolerant sympathy, like she might be dealing with a deluded child. "Your life isn't a wreck. These are just road bumps that are happening all at once. In a year, you'll look back on this and wonder why you ever doubted that things would work out."

"But that's the thing. I'm not really doubting that they will. That's the most absurd part of all this. I should be a tangle of nerves and anxiety, yet I'm...surprisingly calm."

"For the moment," she adds knowingly. "I know how your meltdowns come on. They're like well-orchestrated sneak attacks from a team of deadly covert operatives."

"So you're saying that I really *am* crazy."

"I said no such thing."

"Calm one minute. Under attack the next. That sure sounds crazy."

"No, that's life, Liv. Nothing is perfect *all the time*. If you get perfect *some of the time*, you should thank your lucky stars. And you get perfect *a lot!* A man like yours...all hot and tattooed and delicious...who worships you and tries to put a baby in you every time you're alone together...that sounds pretty damn perfect to me."

"Well, the baby part isn't working out so perfectly, is it?"

Ginger shrugs. "Maybe it is. That whore did all the work. You got off scot-free. Let her have the wrecked vagina and you can just be the sweet, beautiful woman who has all the good stuff. Like the man. And the kid she can send home after the weekend."

"But I *want* the wrecked vagina, Ginger," I moan woefully.

She gasps theatrically. "Bite your tongue! We only get one of these. Take good care of it or you'll end up with a latex allergy and twenty thousand in *Duracell* stock."

I laugh, happily abandoning my distress for her lighter take on life. "Looks like you're faring pretty well. Did you trade in your stock for something...warmer?"

Her blue eyes twinkle merrily. "A lady never tells."

"Good thing you're not a lady. Now spill it, woman."

And she does. Ginger gives me all the romantic, erotic details of her encounter with Gavin. Turns out he's an even hotter Aussie than I thought he'd be. And I had a pretty good idea that he'd be a scorcher.

For the first time since I got the call about Dad, the minutes seem to fly by. When the phone in the otherwise empty little waiting room rings, I jump, throwing a hand up to still my runaway heart.

"See what an amazing distraction that man can be?" Ginger asks, referring to Gavin.

"I see what an amazing distraction *you* can be," I tell her with a smile as I get up and make my way to the phone. I answer according to the location, citing the CV surgery waiting room.

"Ms. Davenport?"

My heart warms. I'll never get tired of being reminded that I belong to Cash. And that he belongs to me.

"Yes?"

"This is Amanda Stein. I'm the circulating nurse for your father's case. I wanted to give you an update."

My heart stutters. "Great. How is he?"

"He did very well. He's off the bypass machine. His heart started functioning on its own right away. The doctor is sewing him up and we'll get him out to a room. I'll call you with a CVICU number when we're ready to transfer him."

A relief so profound it nearly buckles my knees washes through me. I feel the choke of tears clogging my throat despite my earlier sixth sense that everything was going to turn out all right.

"Thank you. Thank you so much."

"My pleasure. I'll be back in touch shortly."

I thank her again and hang up, resisting the urge to go find her and hug her until she can't breathe. I hold onto the edge of the desk for a few seconds, taking deep, grateful breaths until my legs become solid again.

"Everything okay?" Ginger asks from behind me.

"Yes. Very much so. He's done. He made it. They're sewing him up now."

"I knew it!" she exclaims smugly. Ginger isn't really the worrying type.

Carefully, I make my way back to the couch and flop down beside her. She slaps her palm down onto my thigh and wiggles my leg back and forth.

"You know what you need to take the edge off?"

Evidently, my wound-tight state hasn't failed to garner her notice.

"What?" I ask, aware of my silly smile and not caring in the least.

"A spontaneous romp."

I laugh softly, shaking my head. "Is that all you think about?"

Before she answers me, she closes one eye and looks up toward the ceiling for a few seconds. She pretends to be deep in thought. "Yeah. Pretty much."

"I'm glad you didn't bother trying to deny it."

"Eh, why waste a good lie?" She turns to face me fully. "But seriously, you can't tell me that all this talk of sexy sex hasn't helped take your mind off your troubles. Imagine what the real deal could do!"

She's nodding enthusiastically.

"Sex doesn't fix everything, Ginger."

"The hell you say! I'd bet you fifty bucks that Mr. Cash Davenport could loosen you up in a hot minute. I know what you two are like. Rabbits! A couple of damn rabbits! Is there a place you two *haven't* done it?"

Cash and I *do* have an amazing sex life. We always have. He makes me feel things no man has ever made me feel. Part of it is my love for him, but part of it is just because he's so dang good at what he does! It's like he knows my body better than I do and he plays every nerve to the bone, bringing me to peaks I never knew existed.

"See? I know that look. Liv, all you need is a good roll in the hay and you'll be right as rain. Find that handsome hubby and make a baby, dammit!"

Although her approach is crass, as usual, I can't help thinking she might be right. I'm so incredibly relieved that my father is okay, it suddenly seems that anything is possible. Even getting pregnant. And I need to be close to Cash right now. As close as I can possibly get.

I'm aware that Ginger's still talking, but her words fall into a fog in the back of my mind as my husband creeps to the forefront. I see his glistening black eyes, I hear his gravel-and-satin voice, and I'm carried away to a private place that only the two of us visit. Within seconds, I'm consumed. Thoughts of his body gliding into mine, thick and smooth, seem particularly poignant and it isn't long before my cheeks feel as flushed as they might be if he were near.

"You know what, Ginger?" I say, forcing myself back to reality.

"What's that, doll?"

"I think you might be right."

Her smile is positively brilliant, like she's brought me over to the dark side and is especially proud of herself. "Atta girl!"

I pick up my phone to send Cash a text.

EIGHTEEN

Cash

I DON'T know how time got away from me like it did, but I'm driving like a maniac to get back to the hospital. I feel like I let Olivia down by not being there when she got the first bit of good news.

She texted me about an hour ago. She said that the surgery was successful, Darrin was off heart-lung bypass machine and that the doctor was sewing him up. Her tone seemed cheerful and relieved, so *I* was cheerful and relieved. I tried to leave right then, but Gavin had a couple of issues he wanted to discuss. He said it'd take five minutes, but somehow five turned into thirty-five. I'm only minutes from the hospital—finally—but that doesn't make me feel any better.

My phone bleeps with another incoming text and I take a quick second at a red light to look down at it.

Olivia: The doctor came out to talk to me. Dad's prognosis is extremely promising. He won't be awake for a while so I can't see him, but they've moved him to a room in the CVICU.

I tap out a quick reply.

Me: So glad to hear it, babe! I'm almost there. Where are you?

Olivia: Still in the waiting room. Just come here.

Me: Okay. Be there soon. Love you.

Olivia: And I love you, baby.

I smile at the pet name. It speaks to her mood, which seems very good. I'm pleased about that. I was beginning to worry how she'd tolerate all this upheaval in her life on top of not being able to get pregnant. She's strong, though. I don't know why I'm surprised that she bounced back so quickly.

I just hope there's not another storm on the horizon. She needs some calm waters for a little while. This would be enough to drive anyone mad.

As I'm pulling onto the hospital grounds, I get another text. I glance down at it as I'm decelerating on my approach to the parking garage. It's a picture of Olivia's naked chest, shirt unbuttoned, bra pulled down and the fingers of one hand tweaking her nipple.

"Holy shit!" I mutter. My leg jerks and my foot slams on the gas for a second. I have to hit the brake and yank the steering wheel to the left to avoid the concrete barrier that separates the incoming and outgoing lanes of the parking deck. *What the hell is she up to?*

I slide into the first parking spot I can find, one that's not really meant for a full-sized car, but I take it anyway. They can give me a ticket; I don't give a shit. Some things are more important than parking peculiarities. Things like whatever has gotten into my wife. I didn't expect her to bounce back this quickly, but I'm damn sure not gonna gripe about it.

I shift into park and cut the engine, taking a second to reply before I leap from the car and lock it as I'm jogging off toward the hospital entrance.

Me: Are those for me?

Olivia: They could be. So could...other things.

Mother of God! I'm going into a hospital with a dick as stiff as the steel I-beams holding this place together.

Me: What kinds of other things?

Olivia: All sorts of things, starting with these.

There's a long pause before another picture comes in. I'm on the elevator, praying to God that my reception doesn't fail on the way up. And it doesn't. I'm staring at the screen when it comes in. My mouth goes dry as desert dirt when I see it. It's a photo of Olivia's hip, one thumb hooked in the elastic of her lace panties as if she's in the process of pulling them down.

Me: Don't move a muscle. I'll be there in two minutes.

Even if I have to get out and take the stairs, I think to myself, willing the elevator to climb faster. It seems like an eternity has passed before the doors open with a muted swoosh to set me free. I hop out and bound down the hall toward the small waiting room where I left my wife. Of course she's not in here. She can't be if she's sending me half naked pictures.

I text her and note the fine tremor of my hand. God I love Olivia! Only she could do this to me.

Me: I'm in the waiting room. Where are you?

Olivia: Down the hall to the right, last door in the cubbyhole at the end.

I waste no time following her map and finding my way to the single door at the unlit end of the hall. Two supply carts are partially obscuring the door. Bloodflow to my cock increases immediately. We might as well be in a deserted wing.

Me: I'm here.

Olivia: Come on in.

I twist the knob and open the door slowly. There's nothing more than a sink and a toilet and my wife, standing in the center of the small room, smiling.

"You're dressed."

"I didn't want to ruin anything for you. I know how much you like taking my clothes off."

I walk stiffly toward her, clenching and unclenching my fists. How can she still do this to me after all this time? Hell if I know, but I'm not one to complain.

As I draw closer, she backs up to the sink until it hits her in the ass and she has to stop.

"We're gonna be banned from bathrooms before too long. You realize that, don't you?"

She nods, sinking her teeth into her bottom lip.

I reach forward and unbutton her shirt, parting it to reveal her creamy flesh.

"What was it you sent me a picture of, exactly?" I ask. "I think I need you to show me in person."

Her hands are shaking, too, when she reaches up to pull the cups of her bra down to expose her pebbled nipples. She twists and pinches them, her breath escaping her lips in a hushed little huff.

"God, you're beautiful," I tell her on a growl as I bend to take one peak into my mouth. Immediately, she arches her back and fists her fingers in my hair. "Whatever happens next, you just remember that you did this. *You* did this."

I flick open the snap to her shorts and push them down her legs along with her panties. I reach between her thighs and spread her slick folds. She's slippery and ready. *Holy hell!*

"You've been a naughty girl today, it seems," I tell her, thrusting two fingers deep into her. She comes up on her toes and I feel her muscles clench deliciously around my digits.

I look up into her stunningly flushed face and remove my fingers long enough to turn her toward the mirror. "Do you remember our first bathroom?" I ask, moving my hands back to her breasts, rolling her delectable nipples between my thumb and forefingers. She lets her head rest back on my chest, her eyes dark with barely controlled desire.

"Yes," she says breathlessly.

I kiss my way along the curve of her neck and move my right hand to her right leg, lifting until it's resting along the cool ceramic of the sink. The position spreads her wide and my mouth actually waters when I look at the reflection of her slick, swollen pussy.

"Jesus," I mutter, nipping her flesh with my teeth, but unable to take my eyes off her body. I move my palm up the inside of her thigh to her clit. She jerks against me when I pinch it lightly. "I'll kiss that later. I promise," I vow as I rub slow circles over it until she's relaxed again. "I swear to God, Olivia, I've never felt anything like you. I wish you knew what it's like to touch you, to put my fingers in you, my tongue in you, my cock in you. To be inside this perfect body."

"Cash, please," she moans, moving her hips against my hand.

"Unzip me," I tell her, watching as my middle finger disappears into her and then reappears slick with her need. I flex my hips into her when I feel her fumbling with my fly and I can't help groaning when her strong fingers wind around me.

"Now give me your hand," I instruct, knowing I'll probably lose it as soon as I plunge into her. But I don't care. We're going to see this through the right way.

Olivia brings her hand to mine and I take her fingers and press them into her along with mine. I force them deep and then bring them back out to massage her rigid clit. I work them faster and faster until her breath is coming in short bursts. She's close. I can practically feel it coming.

I release her nipple and drag my other hand between us. I push her forward with my chest until her ass is pushed up and out. I pause long enough to find her eyes in the mirror. They're half closed and her mouth is half open. I take a deep breath and ease into her as slowly as I can. Her body clutches snugly around the thickness of my cock and I have to grit my teeth to keep control.

"Christ almighty, you're so hot. And I'm so hard. Can you feel that?" I ask, moving her fingers around to form a V around the base of me, where our bodies join. I pull out and ease back in, shuddering when her fingers slip and slide and tighten around me.

She moves, rubbing her wetness over her clit and then back down around my cock just as I'm pulling out. Her muscles clamp. Her breath hitches. And when I slam back into her, the first spasm hits, pulling me right over the edge with her.

"Cash, oh God!"

Thought abandons me. Finesse deserts me. I sink my fingers into the flesh of her hips, I grip her as tight as I can and I jackhammer my body into hers. I'm vaguely aware of her screaming my name, of that deep sense of satisfaction I always feel when she comes apart so utterly for me. But it's partly lost in the passion that's riding me like a vicious habit I never want to kick. When I explode into her, I have to reach around with one hand to steady myself against the sink just so that I don't topple us both and have us end up on the floor.

I'm quiet for exactly seven heartbeats when I feel it. Come. Hers, mine…it eases from within her to run down my balls. Just like I told her it would that first time in the bathroom at Tad's Sports Bar and Grill, all those months ago.

I rally enough to pull out and ram my body up into hers one last time, hoping against hope that we can create a life this day. I know there is nothing I could do to make my wife happier. And that's all I want out of *my* life—to make Olivia happy.

If you enjoyed this book, please consider leaving a review and recommending it to a friend. You are more powerful than you know. YOU–the words from your mouth, the thoughts from your heart, shared with others, can move mountains. You make a huge difference in the life of an author. You have in mine. You do every day, which brings me to my gratitude, my overwhelming, heartfelt gratitude.

A few times in life, I've found myself in a position of such love and appreciation that saying THANK YOU seems trite, like it's just not enough. That is the position that I find myself in now when it comes to you, my readers. You are the sole reason that my dream of being a writer has come true and your encouragement keeps me going. It brings me unimaginable pleasure to hear that you love my work, that it has touched you in some way, that it has made life seem a little bit better for having read it. So it is from the depths of my soul, from the very bottom of my heart that I say I simply cannot THANK YOU enough, which I say a lot of in this blog post.

ALWAYS WITH YOU, Part One

For the full post, visit my blog at http://mleightonbooks.blogspot.com. You can sign up for my newsletter or find me on Facebook, Twitter, Instagram or Goodreads via my website, www.mleightonbooks.com

ABOUT THE AUTHOR

New York Times and *USA Today* Bestselling Author, M. Leighton, is a native of Ohio. She relocated to the warmer climates of the South, where she can be near the water all summer and miss the snow all winter. Possessed of an overactive imagination from early in her childhood, Michelle finally found an acceptable outlet for her fantastical visions: literary fiction. Having written over a dozen novels, these days Michelle enjoys letting her mind wander to more romantic settings with sexy Southern guys, much like the one she married and the ones you'll find in her latest books. When her thoughts aren't roaming in that direction, she'll be riding wild horses, skiing the slopes of Aspen or scuba diving with a hot rock star, all without leaving the cozy comfort of her office.

<u>YA and PARANORMAL</u>

Fragile

Madly
Madly & the Jackal
Madly & Wolfhardt

Blood Like Poison: For the Love of a Vampire
Blood Like Poison: Destined for a Vampire
Blood Like Poison: To Kill an Angel

The Reaping
The Reckoning

Gravity
Caterpillar
Wiccan
Beginnings: An M. Leighton Anthology

Made in the USA
San Bernardino, CA
14 December 2015